For Darren and
Mark, who didn't
have a bed
R.P.

First published 2012 by
Macmillan Children's Books
a division of Macmillan Publishers Limited
20 New Wharf Road, London N1 9RR
Basingstoke and Oxford
Associated companies throughout the world
www.panmacmillan.com

ISBN: 978-0-230-74764-7 (HB) ISBN: 978-0-230-74768-5 (PB)
Text and illustrations copyright © Rebecca Patterson 2012
Moral rights asserted.

1 3 5 7 9 8 6 4 2

A CIP catalogue record for this book
is available from the British Library.

Printed in China

NOT ON A SCHOOL NIGHT!

Rebecca Patterson

MACMILLAN
CHILDREN'S
BOOKS

At bedtime on Monday, Daddy tucks us in, reads us a story and says goodnight.

But . . .

. . . we don't want to sleep!

We are SUPER BOY and
LITTLE FLASH —

until Mummy comes up
and says, "NOT ON
A SCHOOL NIGHT!"

After lights out on Tuesday, we put on our silly slippers and are Triceratops.

But Daddy comes up and tells us to "STOP ALL THIS ROARING!"

Wednesday bedtime is fun!
We pile EVERYTHING up to do . . .

THE
BIG
JUMP!

And
we
jump,

and jump,

and jump,

and jump again.

"Who is doing all this thudding?" says Mummy.
I say, "I have no idea! We are fast asleep."
And we snore.

On Thursday night we are EXTRA quiet.

We dress up in our bed things.

I am King Pillow,

and my brother is Mr Duvet Slug.

We laugh our heads off . . .

until Mum shouts, "GO TO SLEEP NOW!"

And guess what my brother does?
HE GOES TO SLEEP!

And I am the ONLY person awake in my WHOLE HOUSE!

So I go to sleep, super quick!

But now it's Friday.
Friday nights are special.

We are allowed to
eat tea in our den.

Friday night is **NOT** a school night!

We stay up late and watch TV.

Friday night is fun!

It is almost
as good as . . .

Saturday morning!